STERLING CHILDREN'S BOOKS
New York

An Imprint of Sterling Publishing
387 Park Avenue South
New York, NY 10016

STERLING CHILDREN'S BOOKS and the distinctive Sterling Children's Books
logo are trademarks of Sterling Publishing Co., Inc.

© 2013 by Sterling Publishing Co., Inc.
Design by Jennifer Browning

ISBN 978-1-4027-8351-7

Library of Congress Cataloging-in-Publication Data Available

Distributed in Canada by Sterling Publishing
c/o Canadian Manda Group, 165 Dufferin Street
Toronto, Ontario, Canada M6K 3H6
Distributed in the United Kingdom by GMC Distribution Services
Castle Place, 166 High Street, Lewes, East Sussex, England BN7 1XU
Distributed in Australia by Capricorn Link (Australia) Pty. Ltd.
P.O. Box 704, Windsor, NSW 2756, Australia

For information about custom editions, special sales, and premium and corporate
purchases, please contact Sterling Special Sales at 800-805-5489
or specialsales@sterlingpublishing.com.

Printed in China
Lot #:
2 4 6 8 10 9 7 5 3 1
07/13

www.sterlingpublishing.com/kids

SILVER PENNY STORIES

The Steadfast Tin Soldier

Told by Kathleen Olmstead
Illustrated by Marcos Calo

Once upon a time, there were twenty-four tin soldiers. They wore red uniforms and tall hats. They all stood in a perfectly straight line.

When it was time to finish the last soldier, the toymaker ran out of tin. As a result, the last soldier had only one leg. But he stood just as tall and steady as the other soldiers.

The soldier lived in a playroom with other toys. A cardboard castle stood across from him. It was large, with many tall towers. A doll was standing in the doorway.

The doll was a ballerina. Her skirt was made of pink, puffy silk. She wore a bright blue ribbon in her hair. The tin soldier thought she was beautiful.

The ballerina's arms were stretched in front of her. The tin soldier thought she was reaching toward him. One of her legs was lifted up behind her, so she stood on only one leg.

We are perfect for each other, the tin soldier thought. *I hope someday she will marry me.*

At night, when the children were asleep, the toys came alive. The room was filled with music and games. The toys played, danced, and laughed with each other.

But the tin solder did not speak.
The ballerina did not speak. Neither
moved from their post. They only
watched each other from across
the room.

One morning, a child placed the tin soldier near a window. A sudden gust of wind blew, and the soldier fell outside.

He landed in the garden. It was
raining very hard. Two boys found him.

"Look, a tin soldier!" one said.
"Let's make him a boat."

They folded some paper to make
a tiny boat. They put the tin soldier
inside. A little stream was flowing
down the road at the end of the
garden. The boys put the boat
in the water.

The rain kept getting stronger. The tin soldier stood straight and steady in the boat. He floated down the street into a rain gutter.

It was very dark inside the gutter. The tin soldier could not see much around him. The tiny boat traveled for a long time.

The tiny boat shot out of the gutter into a lake. The boat filled up with water and began to sink. As always, the tin soldier stood straight and steady.

A fish swam up to the tin soldier and swallowed him in one gulp. It was very dark inside the fish. There was nothing to do but wait.

A long time passed. He heard strange noises outside the fish. A bright light hit the toy soldier. The fish was cut open. The tin soldier was free.

What a surprise! The tin soldier was back in his old house. The cook grabbed him and ran to show the children.

The tin soldier was glad to be home. The ballerina stood in her spot, one leg behind and arms stretched out. He took his usual place across from her.

One day, for no reason at all, one of the children threw the tin soldier into the fire. A breeze caught the ballerina and she tumbled in after him.

The next morning, the maid found a bright blue ribbon in the ashes beside a tiny tin heart. "So beautiful," she said. She placed them side by side on the mantle, where they stayed, together at last.